CW00470613

Ellis Parker Butler

That Pup

Ellis Parker Butler

That Pup

1st Edition | ISBN: 978-3-75239-300-2

Place of Publication: Frankfurt am Main, Germany

Year of Publication: 2020

Outlook Verlag GmbH, Germany.

THAT PUP

By Ellis Parker Butler

Fluff was such a sweet little thing

I. THE EDUCATION OF FLUFF

Murchison, who lives next door to me, wants to get rid of a dog, and if you know of anyone who wants a dog I wish you would let Murchison know. Murchison doesn't need it. He is tired of dogs, anyway. That is just like Murchison. 'Way up in an enthusiasm one day and sick of it the next.

Brownlee—Brownlee lives on the other side of Murchison—remembers when Murchison got the dog. It was the queerest thing, so Murchison says, you ever heard of. Here came the express wagon—Adams' Express Company's wagon—and delivered the dog. The name was all right—"C. P. Murchison, Gallatin, Iowa"—and the charges were paid. The charges were $2.80, and paid, and the dog had been shipped from New York. Think of that! Twelve hundred miles in a box, with a can of condensed milk tied to the box and "Please feed" written on it.

Fluff was such a sweet little thing

When Murchison came home to dinner, there was the dog. At first Murchison was pleased; then he was surprised; then he was worried. He hadn't ordered a dog. The more he thought about it the more he worried.

"If I could just *think* who sent it," he said to Brownlee, "then I would know who sent it; but I can't think. It is evidently a valuable dog. I can see that. People don't send cheap, inferior dogs twelve hundred miles. But I can't *think* who sent it."

"What worries me," he said to Brownlee another time, "is who sent it. I can't *imagine* who would send me a dog from New York. I know so many people, and, like as not, some influential friend of mine has meant to make me a nice present, and now he is probably mad because I haven't acknowledged it. I'd like to know what he thinks of me about now!"

It almost worried him sick. Murchison never did care for dogs, but when a man is presented with a valuable dog, all the way from New York, with $2.80 charges paid, he simply *has* to admire that dog. So Murchison got into the habit of admiring the dog, and so did Mrs. Murchison. From what they tell me, it was rather a nice dog in its infancy, for it was only a pup then. Infant dogs have a habit of being pups.

As near as I could gather from what Murchison and Mrs. Murchison told me, it was a little, fluffy, yellow ball, with bright eyes and ever-moving tail. It was the kind of a dog that bounces around like a rubber ball, and eats the evening newspaper, and rolls down the porch steps with short, little squawks of surprise, and lies down on its back with its four legs in the air whenever a bigger dog comes near. In color it was something like a camel, but a little redder where the hair was long, and its hair was like beaver fur—soft and woolly inside, with a few long hairs that were not so soft. It was so little and fluffy that Mrs. Murchison called it Fluff. Pretty name for a soft, little dog is Fluff.

"If I only *knew* who sent that dog," Murchison used to say to Brownlee, "I would like to make some return. I'd send him a barrel of my best melons, express paid, if it cost me five dollars!"

Murchison was in the produce business, and he knew all about melons, but not so much about dogs. Of course he could tell a dog from a cat, and a few things of that sort, but Brownlee was the real dog man. Brownlee had two Irish pointers or setters—I forget which they were; the black dogs with the long, floppy ears. I don't know much about dogs myself. I hate dogs.

Brownlee knows a great deal about dogs. He isn't one of the book-taught sort; he knows dogs by instinct. As soon as he sees a dog he can make a guess at its breed, and out our way that is a pretty good test, for Gallatin dogs are rather cosmopolitan. That is what makes good stock in men—Scotch grandmother and German grandfather on one side and English grandmother and Swedish grandfather on the other—and I don't see why the same isn't true of dogs. There are numbers of dogs in Gallatin that can trace their ancestry through nearly every breed of dog that ever lived, and Brownlee can look at any one of them and immediately guess at its formula—one part Spitz, three parts greyhound, two parts collie, and so on. I have heard him guess more kinds of dog than I ever knew existed.

As soon as he saw Murchison's dog he guessed it was a pure bred Shepherd with a trace of Eskimo. Massett, who thinks he knows as much about dogs as Brownlee does, didn't believe it. The moment he saw the pup he said it was a pedigree dog, half St. Bernard and half Spitz.

Brownlee and Massett used to sit on Murchison's steps after supper and point out the proofs to each other. They would argue for hours.

"All right, Massett," Brownlee would say, "but you can't fool *me*. I Look at that nose! If that isn't a Shepherd nose, I'll eat it. And see that tail! Did you ever see a tail like that on a Spitz? That is an Eskimo tail as sure as I am a foot high."

"Tail fiddlesticks!" Massett would reply. "You can't tell anything by a pup's tail. Look at his ears! *There* is St. Bernard for you! And see his lower jaw. Isn't that Spitz? I'll leave it to Murchison. Isn't that lower jaw Spitz, Murchison?"

Then all three would tackle the puppy and open its mouth and feel its jaw, and the pup would wriggle and squeak, and back away, opening and shutting its mouth to see if its works had been damaged.

"All right!" Brownlee would say. "You wait a year or two and you'll see!"

About three months later the pup was as big as an ordinary full-grown dog, and his coat looked like a compromise between a calfskin and one of these hairbrush door mats you use to wipe your feet on in muddy weather. He did not look like the same pup. He was long limbed and awkward and useless, and homely as a shopworn fifty-cent yellow plush manicure set. Murchison began to feel that he didn't really need a dog, but Brownlee was as enthusiastic as ever. He would go over to Murchison's fairly oozing dog knowledge.

"I'll tell you what that dog is," he would say. "That dog is a cross between a Great Dane and an English Deerhound. You've got a very valuable dog there, Murchison, a very valuable dog. He comes of fine stock on both sides, and it is a cross you don't often see. I never saw it, and I've seen all kinds of crossed dogs."

Then Massett would drop in and walk around the dog admiringly for a few minutes and absorb his beauties.

"Murchison," he would say, "do you know what that dog is? That dog is a pure cross between a Siberian wolfhound and a Newfoundland. You treat that dog right and you'll have a fortune in him. Why, a pure Siberian wolfhound is worth a thousand dollars, and a good—a really good Newfoundland, mind you—is worth two thousand, and you've got both in one dog. That's three thousand dollars' worth of dog!"

In the next six months Fluff grew. He broadened out and lengthened and heightened, and every day or two Brownlee or Massett would discover a new strain of dog in him. They pointed out to Murchison all the marks by which

6

he could tell the different kinds of dog that were combined in Fluff, and every time they discovered a new one they held a sort of jubilee, and bragged and swelled their chests. They seemed to spend all their time thinking up odd and strange kinds of dog that Fluff had in him. Brownlee discovered the traces of Cuban bloodhound, Kamtchatka hound, beagle, Brague de Bengale, and Thibet mastiff, but Massett first traced the stag-hound, Turkoman watchdog, Dachshund, and Harrier in him.

They held a sort of a jubilee

Murchison, not being a doggish man, never claimed to have noticed any of these family resemblances, and never said what he thought the dog really was until a month or two later, when he gave it as his opinion that the dog was a cross between a wolf, a Shetland pony, and hyena. It was about that time that Fluff had to be chained. He had begun to eat other dogs, and children and chickens. The first night Murchison chained him to his kennel Fluff walked half a mile, taking the kennel along, and then only stopped because the kennel got tangled with a lamp-post. The man who brought him home claimed that Fluff was nearly asphyxiated when he found him; said he gnawed half through the lamp-post, and that gas got in his lungs, but this was not true. Murchison learned afterwards that it was only a gasoline lamp-post, and a wooden one.

"If there were only some stags around this part of the country," said Massett, "the stag-hound strain in that dog would be mighty valuable. You could rent him out to everybody who wanted to go stag hunting; and you'd have a regular monopoly, because he's the only staghound in this part of the country. And stag hunting would be popular, too, out here, because there are no game laws that interfere with stag hunting in this State. There is no closed season. People could hunt stags all the year round, and you'd have that dog busy every day of the year."

"Yes!" sneered Brownlee, "only there are no stags. And he hasn't any staghound blood in him. Pity there are no Dachs in this State, too, isn't it? Then Murchison could hire his dog at night, too. They hunt Dachs at night, don't they, Massett? Only there is no Dachshund blood in him, either. If there was, and if there were a few Dachs-"

Massett was mad.

"Yes!" he cried. "And you, with your Cuban bloodhound strain! I suppose if it was the open season for Cubans, you'd go out with the dog and tree a few! Or put on snowshoes and follow the Kamtchat to his icy lair!" Brownlee doesn't get mad easily.

"Murchison," he said, "leaving out Mas-sett's dreary nonsense about staghounds, I can tell you that dog would make the finest duck dog in the State. He's got all the points for a good duck dog, and I ought to know for I have two of the best duck dogs that ever lived. All he needs is training. If you will train him right you'll have a mighty valuable dog."

"But I don't hunt ducks," said Murchison, "and I don't know how to train even a lap-dog."

"You let me attend to his education," said Brownlee. "I just want to show Massett here that I know a dog when I see one. I'll show Massett the finest duck dog he ever saw when I get through with Fluff."

So he went over and got his shotgun, just to give Fluff his first lesson. The first thing a duck dog must learn is not to be afraid of a gun, and Brownlee said that if a dog first learned about guns right at his home he was not so apt to be afraid of them. He said that if a dog heard a gun for the first time when he was away from home and in strange surroundings he was quite right to be surprised and startled, but if he heard it in the bosom of his family, with all his friends calmly seated about, he would think it was a natural thing, and accept it as such.

So Brownlee put a shell in his gun and Mas-sett and Murchison sat on the porch steps and pretended to be uninterested and normal, and Brownlee stood up and aimed the gun in the air. Fluff was eating a bone, but Brownlee spoke to him and he looked up, and Brownlee pulled the trigger. It seemed about five minutes before Fluff struck the ground, he jumped so high when the gun was fired, and then he started north by northeast at about sixty miles an hour. He came back all right, three weeks later, but his tail was still between his legs.

He came back all right, three weeks later

Brownlee didn't feel the least discouraged. He said he saw now that the whole principle of what he had done was wrong; that no dog with any brains whatever could be anything but frightened to hear a gun shot off right in the bosom of his family. That was no place to fire a gun. He said Fluff evidently thought the whole lot of us were crazy, and ran in fear of his life, thinking we were insane and might shoot him next. He said the thing to do was to take the shotgun into its natural surroundings and let Fluff learn to love it there. He pictured Fluff enjoying the sound of the gun when he heard it at the edge of the lake.

Murchison never hunted ducks, but as Fluff was his dog, he went with Brownlee, and of course Massett went. Massett wanted to see the failure. He said he wished stags were as plentiful as ducks, and he would show Brownlee!

Fluff was a strong dog—he seemed to have a strain of ox in him, so far as strength went—and as long as he saw the gun he insisted that he would stay at home; but when Brownlee wrapped the gun in brown paper so it looked like a big parcel from the meat shop, the horse that they had hitched to the buck-board was able to drag Fluff along without straining itself. Fluff was fastened to the rear axle with a chain.

When they reached Duck Lake, Brownlee untied Fluff and patted him, and then unwrapped the gun. Fluff gave one pained glance and made the six-mile run home in seven minutes without stopping. He was home before Brownlee could think of anything to say, and he went so far into his kennel that Murchison had to take off the boards at the back to find him that night.

"That's nothing," was what Brownlee said when he did speak; "young dogs are often that way. Gun fright. They have to be gun broken. You come out to-morrow, and I'll show you how a man who really knows how to handle a dog does the trick."

The next day, when Fluff saw the buck-board he went into his kennel, and they couldn't pry him out with the hoe-handle. He connected buckboards and guns in his mind, so Brownlee borrowed the butcher's delivery wagon, and they drove to Wild Lake. It was seven miles, but Fluff seemed more willing to go in that direction than toward Duck Lake. He did not seem to care to go to Duck Lake at all.

"Now, then," said Brownlee, "I'll show you the intelligent way to handle a dog. I'll prove to him that he has nothing to fear, that I am his comrade and friend. And at the same time," he said, "I'll not have him running off home and spoiling our day's sport."

So he took the chain and fastened it around his waist, and then he sat down and talked to Fluff like an old friend, and got him in a playful mood. Then he had Murchison get the gun out of the wagon and lay it on the ground about twenty feet off. It was wrapped in brown paper.

Brownlee talked to Fluff and told him what fine sport duck hunting is, and then, as if by chance, he got on his hands and knees and crawled toward the gun. Fluff hung back a little, but the chain just coaxed him a little, too, and they edged up to the gun, and Brownlee pretended to discover it unexpectedly.

"Well, well!" he said. "What's this?"

Fluff nosed up to it and sniffed it, and then went at it as if it was Massett's cat. That Brownlee had wrapped a beefsteak around the gun, inside the paper, and Fluff tore off the paper and ate the steak, and Brownlee winked at Murchison.

"I declare," he said, "if here isn't a gun! Look at this, Fluff—a gun! Gosh! but we are in luck!"

Would you believe it, that dog sniffed at the gun, and did not fear it in the least? You could have hit him on the head with it and he would not have minded it. He never did mind being hit with small things like guns and ax handles.

Brownlee got up and stood erect.

"You see!" he said proudly. "All a man needs with a dog like this is intelligence. A dog is like a horse. He wants his reason appealed to. Now, if I fire the gun, he may be a little startled, but I have created a faith in me in him. He knows there is nothing dangerous in a gun *as* a gun. He knows I am not afraid of it, so he is not afraid. He realizes that we are chained together, and that proves to him that he need not run unless I run. Now watch."

Brownlee fired the shotgun.

Instantly he started for home. He did not start lazily, like a boy starting to the wood pile, but went promptly and with a dash. His first jump was only ten feet, and we heard him grunt as he landed, but after that he got into his stride and made fourteen feet each jump. He was bent forward a good deal in the middle, where the chain was, and in many ways he was not as graceful as a professional cinder-path track runner, but, in running, the main thing is to cover the ground rapidly. Brownlee did that.

Massett said it was a bad start. He said it was all right to start a hundred-yard dash that way, but for a long-distance run—a run of seven miles across country—the start was too impetuous; that it showed a lack of generalship,

11

and that when it came to the finish the affair would be tame; but it wasn't.

Brownlee said afterwards that there wasn't a tame moment in the entire seven miles. It was rather more wild than tame. He felt right from the start that the finish would be sensational, unless the chain cut him quite in two, and it didn't. He said that when the chain had cut as far as his spinal column it could go no farther, and it stopped and clung there, but it was the only thing that did stop, except his breath. It was several years later that I first met Brownlee, and he was still breathing hard, like a man who has just been running rapidly. Brownlee says when he shuts his eyes his legs still seem to be going.

The first mile was through underbrush, and that was lucky, for the underbrush removed most of Brownlee's clothing, and put him in better running weight, but at the mile and a quarter they struck the road. He said at two miles he thought he might be overexercising the dog and maybe he had better stop, but the dog seemed anxious to get home so he didn't stop there. He said that at three miles he was sure the dog was overdoing, and that with his knowledge of dogs he was perfectly able to stop a running dog in its own length if he could speak to it, but he couldn't speak to this dog for two reasons. One was that he couldn't overtake the dog and the other was that all the speak was yanked out of him.

When they reached five miles the dog seemed to think they were taking too much time to get home, and let out a few more laps of speed, and it was right there that Brownlee decided that Fluff had some greyhound blood in him.

He said that when they reached town he felt as if he would have been glad to stop at his own house and lie down for awhile, but the dog didn't want to, and so they went on; but that he ought to be thankful that the dog was willing to stop at that town at all. The next town was twelve miles farther on, and the roads were bad. But the dog turned into Murchison's yard and went right into his kennel.

When Murchison and Massett got home, an hour or so later, after driving the horse all the way at a gallop, they found old Gregg, the carpenter, prying the roof off the kennel. You see, Murchison had knocked the rear out of the kennel the day before, and so when the dog aimed for the front he went straight through, and as Brownlee was built more perpendicular than the dog, Brownlee didn't go quite through. He went in something like doubling up a dollar bill to put it into a thimble. I don't suppose anyone would want to double up a dollar bill to put it into a thimble, but neither did Brownlee want to be doubled up and put into the kennel. It was the dog's thought. So they had to take the kennel roof off.

When they got Brownlee out they laid him on the grass, and covered him up with a porch rug, and let him lie there a couple of hours to pant, for that seemed what he wanted to do just then. It was the longest period Brownlee ever spent awake without talking about dog.

Murchison and Massett and old Gregg and twenty-six informal guests stood around and gazed at Brownlee panting. Presently Brownlee was able to gasp out a few words.

"Murchison," he gasped, "Murchison, if you just had that dog in Florence —or wherever it is they race dogs—you'd have a fortune."

He panted awhile, and then gasped out:

"He's a great runner; a phenomenal runner!"

He had to pant more, and then he gasped with pride:

"But I wasn't three feet behind him all the way!"

II. GETTING RID OF FLUFF

So after that Murchison decided to get rid of Fluff. He told me that he had never really-wanted a dog, anyway, but that when a dog is sent, all the way from New York, anonymously, with $2.80 charges paid, it is hard to cast the dog out into the cold world without giving it a trial. So Murchison tried the dog for a few more years, and at last he decided he would have to get rid of him. He came over and spoke to me about it, because I had just moved in next door.

"Do you like dogs?" he asked, and that was the first word of conversation I ever had with Murchison. I told him frankly that I did not like dogs, and that my wife did not like them, and Murchison seemed more pleased than if I had offered him a thousand dollars.

"Now, I am glad of that," he said, "for Mrs. Murchison and I hate dogs. If you do not like dogs, I will get rid of Fluff. I made up my mind several years ago to get rid of Fluff, but when I heard you were going to move into this house, I decided not to get rid of him until I knew whether you liked dogs or not. I told Mrs. Murchison that if we got rid of Fluff before you came, and then found that you loved dogs and owned one, you might take our getting rid of Fluff as a hint that your dog was distasteful to us, and it might hurt your feelings. And Mrs. Murchison said that if you had a dog, your dog might feel lonely in a strange place and might like to have Fluff to play with until your dog got used to the neighborhood. So we did not get rid of him; but if you do not like dogs we will get rid of him right away."

I told Murchison that I saw he was the kind of a neighbor a man liked to have, and that it was kind of him to offer to get rid of Fluff, but that he mustn't do so just on our account.

I said that if he wanted to keep the dog, he had better do so.

"Now, that is kind of you," said Murchison, "but we would really rather get rid of him. I decided several years ago that I would get rid of him, but Brownlee likes dogs, and took an interest in Fluff, and wanted to make a bird dog of him, so we kept Fluff for his sake. But now Brownlee is tired of making a bird dog of him. He says Fluff is too strong to make a good bird dog, and not strong enough to rent out as a horse, and he is willing I should get rid of him. He says he is anxious for me to get rid of him as soon as I can."

When I saw Fluff I agreed with Brownlee. At the first glance I saw that

Fluff was a failure as a dog, and that to make a good camel he needed a shorter neck and more hump, but he had the general appearance of an amateur camel. He looked as if some one who had never seen a dog, but had heard of one, had started out to make a dog, and got to thinking of a camel every once in a while, and had tried to show me Fluff that day worked in parts of what he thought a camel was like with what he thought a dog was like, and then— when the job was about done—had decided it was a failure, and had just finished it up any way, sticking on the meanest and cheapest hair he could find, and getting most of it on wrong side to.

But the cheap hair did not matter much. Murchison and Brownlee showed me the place where Fluff had worn most of it off the ridge pole of his back crawling under the porch. He tried to show me Fluff that day, but it was so dark under the porch that I could not tell which was Fluff and which was simply underneathness of porch. But from what Brownlee told me that day, I knew that Fluff had suffered a permanent dislocation of the spirits. He told me he had taken Fluff out to make a duck dog of him, and that all the duck Fluff was interested in was to duck when he saw a gun, and that after he had heard a gun fired once or twice he had become sad and dejected, and had acquired a permanently ingrowing tail, and an expression of face like a coyote, but more mournful. He had acquired a habit of carrying his head down and forward, as if he was about to lay it on the headsman's block, and knew he deserved that and more, and the sooner it was over the better. He couldn't even scratch fleas correctly. Brownlee said that when he met a flea in the road he would not even go around it, but would stoop down like a camel to let the flea get aboard. He was that kind of a dog. He was the most discouraged dog I ever knew.

He tried to show me Fluff that day

The next day I was putting down the carpet in the back bedroom, when in came Murchison.

"I came over to speak to you about Fluff," he said. "I am afraid he must have annoyed you last night. I suppose you heard him howl?"

"Yes, Murchison," I said, "I did hear him. I never knew a dog could howl so loud and long as that. He must have been very ill."

"Oh, no!" said Murchison cheerfully. "That is the way he always howls. That is one of the reasons I have decided to get rid of Fluff. But it is a great deal worse for us than it is for you. The air inlet of our furnace is at the side of the house just where Fluff puts his head when he howls, and the register in our room is right at the head of our bed. So his howl goes in at the inlet and down through the furnace and up the furnace pipes, and is delivered right in our room, just as clear and strong as if he was in the room. That is one reason I have fully decided to get rid of Fluff. It would not be so bad if we had only one register in our house, but we have ten, and when Fluff howls, his voice is delivered by all ten registers, so it is just as if we had ten Fluffs in the house at one time. And ten howls like Fluff's are too much. Even Brownlee says so." I told Murchison that I agreed with Brownlee perfectly. Fluff had a bad howl. It sounded as if Cruel Fate, with spikes in his shoes, had stepped on Fluff's inmost soul, and then jogged up and down on the tenderest spot, and Fluff was trying to reproduce his feelings in vocal exercises. It sounded like a cheap phonograph giving a symphony in the key of woe minor, with a megaphone attachment and bad places in the record. Judging by his voice, the machine needed a new needle. But the megaphone attachment was all right.

Brownlee—who knows all about dogs—said that he knew what was the matter with Fluff. He said Fluff had a very high-grade musical temperament, and that he longed to be the Caruso of dogs. He said that he could see that all through his bright and hopeful puppyhood he had looked forward to being a great singer, with a Wagner repertoire and tremolo stops in his song organ, and that he had early set his aim at perfection. He said Fluff was that kind of a dog, and that when he saw what his voice had turned out to be he was dissatisfied, and became morbid. He said that any dog that had a voice like Fluff's had a right to be dissatisfied with it—he would be dissatisfied himself with that voice. He said he did not wonder that Fluff slunk around all day, feeling he was no good on earth, and that he could understand that when night came and everything was still, so that Fluff could judge of the purity of his tonal quality better, he would pull out his voice, and tune it up and look it over and try it again, hoping it had improved since he tried it last. Brownlee said it never had improved, and that was what made Fluff's howl so mournful —it was full of tears. He said Fluff would go to G flat and B flat and D flat, and so on until he struck a note he felt he was pretty good at, and then he would cling to that note and weep it full of tears.

He would cling to that note

He asked Murchison if he hadn't noticed that the howl was sort of damp and salty from the tears, but Murchison said he hadn't noticed the dampness. He said it probably got dried out of the howl before it readied him, coming through the furnace. Then Brownlee said that if there was only some way of regulating Fluff, so that he could be turned on and off, Murchison would have a fortune in him: he could turn his howl off when people wanted to be cheerful, and then, when a time of great national woe occurred, Murchison could turn Fluff on and set him going. He said he never heard anything in his life that came so near expressing in sound a great national woe as Fluff's howl did. He said Fluff might lack finish in tonal quality, but that in woe quality he was a master: he was stuffed so full of woe quality that it oozed out of his pores. He said he always thought what a pity it was for dogs like Fluff that people preferred cheerful songs like "Annie Rooney" and "Waltz me around again, Willie" to the nobler woe operas. He said he had tried to like good music himself, but it was no use: whenever he heard Fluff sing, he felt that Murchison ought to get rid of Fluff. Then Murchison said that was just what he was going to do. What he wanted to talk about was how to get rid of Fluff.

But I am getting too far ahead of my story. Whenever I get to talking about the howl of Fluff, I find I wander on for hours at a time.

It takes hours of talk to explain just what a mean howl Fluff had.

But as I was saying, Murchison came over while I was putting down the carpet in my back bedroom, and told me he had fully decided to get rid of Fluff.

"I have fully decided to get rid of him," he said, "and the only thing that bothers me is how to get rid of him."

"Give him away," I suggested.

"That's a good idea!" said Murchison gratefully. "That's the very idea that occurred to me when I first thought of getting rid of Fluff. It is an idea that just matches Fluff all over. That is just the kind of dog Fluff is. If ever a dog was made to give away, Fluff was made for it. The more I think about him and look at him and study him, the surer I am that the only thing he is good for is to give away."

Then he shook his head and sighed.

"The only trouble," he said, "is that Fluff *is* the give-away kind of dog. That is the only kind you can't give away. There is only one time of the year that a person can make presents of things that are good for nothing but to give away, and that is at Christmas. Now, I might—"

"Murchison," I said, laying my tack hammer on the floor and standing up, "you don't mean to keep that infernal, howling beast until Christmas, do you? If you do, I shall stop putting down this carpet. I shall pull out the tacks that are already in and move elsewhere. Why, this is only the first of May, and if I have to sleep—if I have to keep awake every night and listen to that animated foghorn drag his raw soul over the teeth of a rusty harrow—I shall go crazy. Can't you think of some one that is going to have a birthday sooner than that?"

"I wish I could," said Murchison wistfully, "but I can't. I want to get rid of Fluff, and so does Brownlee, and so does Massett, but I can't think of a way to get rid of him, and neither can they."

"Murchison," I said, with some asperity, for I hate a man who trifles, "if I really thought you and Brownlee and Massett were as stupid as all that, I would be sorry I moved into this neighborhood, but I don't believe it. I believe you do not mean to get rid of Fluff. I believe you and Brownlee and Massett want to keep him. If you wanted to get rid of him, you could do it the same way you got him."

"That's an excellent idea!" exclaimed Murchison. "That is one of the best ideas I ever heard, and I would go and do it if I hadn't done it so often already. As soon as Brownlee suggested that idea I did it. I sent Fluff by express to a man—to John Smith—at Worcester, Mass., and when Fluff came back I had to pay $8.55 charges. But I didn't begrudge the money. The trip did Fluff a world of good—it strengthened his voice, and made him broader-minded. I tell you," he said enthusiastically, "there's nothing like travel for broadening the mind! Look at Fluff! Maybe he don't show it, but that dog's mind is so broadened by travel that if he was turned loose in Alaska he would find his way home. When I found his mind was getting so tremendously broad I stopped sending him to places. Brownlee—Brownlee knows all about dogs—said it would not hurt Fluff a bit; he said a dog's mind could not get too broad, and that as far as he was concerned he would just like to see once how broad-minded a dog could become; he would like to have Fluff sent out by express every time he came back. He told me it was an interesting experiment—that so far as he knew it had never been tried before—and that the thing I ought to do was to keep Fluff traveling all the time. He said that so far as he knew it was the only way to get rid of Fluff; that some time while he was traveling around in the express car there might be a wreck, and we would be rid of Fluff; and if there wasn't a wreck, it would be interesting to see what effect constant travel would have on a coarse dog. He said I might find after a year or two that I had the most cultured dog in the United States. Brownlee was willing to have me send Fluff anywhere. He suggested a lot of good places to send dogs, but he didn't care enough about dog culture to help pay the express charges."

"I see, Murchison," I said scornfully, "I see! You are the kind of a man who would let a little money stand between you and getting rid of a dog like Fluff!

If I had a dog like Fluff, nothing in the world could prevent me from getting rid of him. I only wish, he was my dog."

"Take him!" said Murchison generously; "I make you a full and free present of him. You can have that dog absolutely and wholly. He is yours."

"I will take the dog," I said haughtily, "not because I really want a dog, nor because I hanker for that particular dog, but because I can see that you and Brownlee and Massett have been trifling with him. Bring him over in my yard, and I will show you in very short measure how to get rid of Fluff."

That afternoon both Brownlee and Massett called on me. They came and sat on my porch steps, and Murchison came and sat with them, and all three sat and looked at Fluff and talked him over. Every few minutes they would— Brownlee and Massett would—get up and shake hands with Murchison, and congratulate him on having gotten rid of Fluff, and Murchison would blush modestly and say:

"Oh, that is nothing! I always knew I would get rid of him." And there was the dog not five feet from them, tied to my lawn hydrant. I watched and listened to them until I had had enough of it, and then I went into the house and got my shotgun. I loaded it with a good BB shell and went out.

He took the hydrant and the pipe with him

Fluff saw me first. I never saw a dog exhibit such intelligence as Fluff exhibited right then. I suppose travel had broadened him, and probably the hydrant was old and rusted out, anyway. When a man moves into a house he ought to have *all* the plumbing attended to the first thing. Any ordinary, unbroadened dog would have lain down and pulled, but Fluff didn't. First he jumped six feet straight into the air, and that pulled the four feet of hydrant pipe up by the roots, and then he went away. He took the hydrant and the pipe with him, and that might have surprised me, but I saw that he did not know where he was going nor how long he would stay there when he reached the place, and a dog can never tell what will come handy when he is away from home. A hydrant and a piece of iron pipe might be the very thing he would need. So he took them along.

If I had wanted a fountain in my front yard, I could not have got one half as quickly as Fluff furnished that one, and I would never have thought of pulling out the hydrant to make me one. Fluff thought of that—at least Brownlee said he thought of it—but I think all Fluff wanted was to get away. And he got away, and the fountain didn't happen to be attached to the hydrant, so he left it behind. If it had been attached to the hydrant, he would have taken it with him. He was a strong dog.

"There!" said Brownlee, when we had heard the pipe rattle across the Eighth Street bridge—"there is intelligence for you! You ought to be grateful to that dog all your life. *You* didn't know it was against the law to discharge a gun in the city limits, but Fluff did, and he wouldn't wait to see you get into trouble. He has heard us talking about it, Murchison. I tell you travel has broadened that dog! Look what he has saved you," he said to me, "by going away at just the psychological moment. We should have told you about not firing a gun in the city limits. You can't get rid of Fluff that way. It is against the law."

"Yes," said Massett; "and if you knew Fluff as well as we do you would know that he is a dog you can't shoot. He is a wonderful dog. He knows all about guns. Brownlee tried to make a duck dog out of him, and took him out where the ducks were—showed him the ducks—shot a gun at the ducks—and what do you think that dog learned?"

"To run," I said, for I had heard about Brownlee teaching Fluff to retrieve. Brownlee blushed.

"Yes," said Massett, "but that wasn't all. It doesn't take intelligence to make a dog run when he sees a gun, but Fluff did not run like an ordinary dog. He saw the gun and he saw the ducks, and he saw that Brownlee only shot at ducks when they were on the wing. And he thought Brownlee meant to shoot him, so what does he do? Stand still? No; he tries to fly. Gets right up and tries to fly. He thought that was what Brownlee was trying to teach him. He couldn't fly, but he did his best. So whenever Fluff sees a gun, he is on the wing, so to speak. You noticed he was on the wing, didn't you?"

I told him I had noticed it. I said that as far as I could judge, Fluff had a good strong wing. I said I didn't mind losing a little thing like a hydrant and a length or two of pipe, but I was glad I hadn't fastened Fluff to the house—I always liked my house to have a cellar——and it would be just like Fluff to stop flying at some place where there wasn't any cellar.

"Oh," said Massett, "he wouldn't have gone far with the house. A house is a great deal heavier than a hydrant. He would probably have moved the house off the foundation a little, but, judging by the direction Fluff took, the house would have wedged between those two trees, and you would have only lost a piece of the porch, or whatever he was tied to. But the lesson is that you must not try to shoot Fluff unless you are a good wing shot. Unless you can shoot like Davy Crockett, you would be apt to wound Fluff without killing him, and then there *would* be trouble!"

"Yes," said Murchison, "the Prevention of Cruelty to Animals folks. There is only one way in which a dog can be killed according to law in this place, and that is to have the Prevention of Cruelty to Animals folks do it. You send them a letter telling them you have a dog you want killed, and asking them to come and kill it. That is according to law."

"That," I said firmly, "is what I will do."

"It won't do any good," said Murchison sadly; "they never come. This addition to Gallatin is too far from their offices to be handy, and they never come. I have eighteen deaths for Fluff on file at their offices already, and not one of them has killed him. When you have had as much experience with dogs as I have had you will know that the Prevention of Cruelty to them in this town does not include killing them when they live in the suburbs. The only way a dog can die in the suburbs of Gallatin is to die of old age."

"How old is Fluff?" I asked.

"Fluff is a young dog," said Brownlee. "If he had an ordinary dog constitution, he would live fifteen years yet, but he hasn't. He has an extra strong constitution, and I should say he was good for twenty years more. But that isn't what we came over for. We came over to learn how you mean to get rid of Fluff."

"Brownlee," I said, "I shall think up some way to get rid of Fluff. Getting rid of a dog is no task for a mind like mine. But until he returns and gives me back my hydrant, I shall do nothing further. I am not going to bother about getting rid of a dog that is not here to be got rid of."

By the time Fluff returned I had thought out a plan. Murchison had never paid the dog tax on Fluff, and that was the same as condemning him to death if he was ever caught outside of the yard, but when he was outside he could not be caught. He was a hasty mover, and little things such as closed gates never prevented him from entering the yard when in haste. When he did not jump over he could get right through a fence. But to a man of my ability these things are trifles. I knew how to get rid of Fluff. I knew how to have him caught in the street without a license. I chained him there.

Brownlee and Massett and Murchison came and watched me do it. Our street is not much used, and the big stake I drove in the street was not much in the way of passing grocery delivery wagons. I fastened Fluff to the stake with a chain, and then I wrote to the city authorities and complained. I said there was a dog without a license that was continually in front of my house, and I wished it removed; and a week or so later the dog-catcher came around and had a look at Fluff: He walked all around him while Massett and Brownlee and Murchison and I leaned over our gates and looked on. He was not at all what I should have expected a dog-catcher to be, being thin and rather gentlemanly in appearance; and after he had looked Fluff over well he came over and spoke to me. He asked me if Fluff was my dog. I said he was.

"I see!" said the dog-catcher. "And you want to get rid of him. If he was my dog, I would want to get rid of him, too. I have seen lots of dogs, but I never saw one that was like this, and I do not blame you for wanting to part with him. I have had my eye on him for several years, but this is the first opportunity I have had to approach him. Now, however, he seems to have broken all the dog laws. He has not secured a license, and he is in the public highway. It will be my duty to take him up and gently chloroform him as soon as I make sure of one thing."

"Tell me what it is," I said, "and I will help you make sure of ft."

"Thank you," he said, "but I will attend to it," and with that he got on his wagon and drove off. He returned in about an hour.

"I came back," he said, "not because my legal duty compels me, but because I knew you would be anxious. If I owned a dog like that, I would be anxious, too. I can't take that dog."

"Why not?" we all asked.

"Because," he said, "I have been down to the city hall, and I have looked up the records, and I find that the streets of this addition to the city have not been accepted by the city. The titles to the property are so made out that until the city legally accepts the streets, each property owner owns to the middle of the street fronting his property. If you will step out and look, you will see that the dog is on your own property."

The dog is on your own property

"If that is all," I said, "I will move the stake. I will put him on the other side of the street."

"If you would like him any better there," said the dog-catcher, "you can move him, but it would make no difference to me. Then he would be on the private property of the man who owns the property across the street."

"But, my good man," I said, "how *is* a man to get rid of a dog he does not want?"

The dog-catcher frowned.

"That," he said, "seems to be one of the things our lawmakers have not thought of. But whatever you do, I advise you to be careful. Do not try any underhand methods, for now that my attention has been called to the dog, I shall have to watch his future and see that he is not badly used. I am an officer of the Prevention of Cruelty to Animals as well as a dog-catcher, and I warn you to be careful what you do with that dog."

Then he got on his wagon again and drove away.

The next morning I was a nervous wreck, for Fluff had howled all night, and Murchison came over soon after breakfast. He was accompanied by Brownlee and Massett.

"Now, I am the last man in the world to do anything that my neighbors would take offense at," he said, as soon as they were seated on my porch, "and Brownlee and Massett love dogs as few men ever love them; but something has to be done about Fluff. The time has come when we must sleep with our windows open, and neither Massett nor Brownlee nor I got a minute of sleep last night."

"Neither did I," I said.

"That is different entirely," said Murchison. "Fluff is your dog, and if you want to keep a howling dog, you would be inclined to put up with the howl, but we have no interest in the dog at all. We do not own him, and we consider him a nuisance. We have decided to ask you to get rid of him. It is unjust to your neighbors to keep a howling dog. You will have to get rid of Fluff."

"Exactly!" said Massett. "For ten nights I have not slept a wink, and neither has Murchison, nor has Brownlee—"

"Nor I," I added.

"Exactly!" said Massett. "And four men going without sleep for ten nights is equal to one man going without sleep forty nights, which would kill any man. Practically, Fluff has killed a man, and is a murderer, and as you are responsible for him, it is the same as if you were a murderer yourself; and as you were one of the four who did not sleep, you may also be said to have committed suicide. But we do not mean to give you into the hands of the law until we have remonstrated with you. But we feel deeply, and the more so because you could easily give us some nights of sleep in which to recuperate."

"If you can tell me how," I said, "I will gladly do it. I need sleep more at this minute than I ever needed it in my life."

"Very well," said Massett; "just get out your shotgun and show it to Fluff. When he sees the gun he will run. He will take wings like a duck, and while he is away we can get a few nights' rest. That will be something. And if we are not in good condition by that time, you can show him the shotgun again. Why!" he exclaimed, as he grew enthusiastic over his idea, "you can keep Fluff eternally on the wing!"

I felt that I needed a vacation from Fluff. I unchained him and went in to get my shotgun. Then I showed him the shotgun, and we had two good nights of sleep. After that, whenever we felt that we needed a few nights in peace, I just showed Fluff the shotgun and he went away on one of his flying trips.

But it was Brownlee—Brownlee knew all about dogs—who first called my attention to what he called the periodicity of Fluff.

"Now, you would never have noticed it," he said one day when Murchison and I were sitting on my porch with him, "but I did. That is because I have studied dogs. I know all about dogs, and I know Fluff can run. This is because he has greyhound blood in him. With a little wolf. That is why I studied Fluff, and how I came to notice that every time you show him the shotgun he is gone just forty-eight hours. Now, you go and get your shotgun and try it."

So I tried it, and Fluff went away as he always did; and Brownlee sat there bragging about how Fluff could run, and about how wonderful he was himself to have thought of the periodicity of Fluff.

"Did you see how he went?" he asked enthusiastically. "That gait was a thirty-mile-an-hour gait. Why, that dog travels—he travels—" He took out a piece of paper and a pencil and figured it out. "In forty-eight hours he travels fourteen hundred and forty miles! He gets seven hundred and twenty miles from home!"

"It doesn't seem possible," said Murchison. "No," said Brownlee frankly, "it doesn't." He went over his figures again. "But that is figured correctly," he said. "If—but maybe I did not gauge his speed correctly. And I didn't allow for stopping to turn around at the end of the out sprint. What we ought to have on that dog is a pedometer. If I owned a dog like that, the first thing I would get would be a pedometer."

I told Brownlee that if he wished I would give him Fluff, and he could put a pedometer, or anything else, on him; but Brownlee remembered he had some work to do and went home.

But he was right about the periodicity of Fluff. Almost on the minute at the end of forty-eight hours Fluff returned, and Brownlee and Murchison, who were there to receive him, were as pleased as if Fluff had been going away instead of returning.

"That dog," said Brownlee, "is a wonderful animal. If Sir Isaac Newton had that dog, he would have proved something or other of universal value by him.

That dog is plumb full of ratios and things, if we only knew how to get them out of him. I bet if Sir Isaac Newton had had Fluff as long as you have had him he would have had a formula all worked out—$x/y(2xz-dog)=2(4ab-3x)$ or something of that kind, so that anyone with half a knowledge of algebra could figure out the square root of any dog any time of the day or night. I could get up a Law of Dog myself if I had the time, with a dog like Fluff to work on. 'If one dog travels fourteen hundred and forty miles at the sight of a gun, how far would two dogs travel?' All that sort of thing. Stop!" he ejaculated suddenly. "If one dog travels forty-eight hours at the sight of one gun, how far would he travel at the sight of two guns? Murchison," he cried enthusiastically, "I've got it! I've got the fundamental law of periodicity in dogs! Go get your gun," he said to me, "and I will get mine."

How far would he travel at the sight of two guns?

He stopped at the gate long enough to say:

"I tell you, Murchison, we are on the verge of a mighty important discovery —a mighty important discovery! If this thing turns out right, we will be at the root of all dog nature. We will have the great underlying law of scared dogs."

He came back with his shotgun carefully hidden behind him, and then he and I showed Fluff the two guns simultaneously. For one minute Fluff was startled. Then he vanished. All we saw of him as he went was the dust he left in his wake. Massett had come over when Brownlee brought over his gun, and Murchison and I sat and smoked while Massett and Brownlee fought out the periodicity of Fluff. Brownlee said that for two guns Fluff would traverse the same distance as for one, but twice as quickly; but Massett said Brownlee was foolish, and that anyone who knew anything about dogs would know that no dog could go faster than Fluff had gone at the sight of one gun. Massett said Fluff would travel at his regular one-gun speed, but would travel a two-gun distance. He said Fluff would not be back for ninety-six hours. Brownlee said he would be back in forty-eight hours, but both agreed that he would travel twenty-eight hundred and eighty miles. Then Murchison went home and got a map, and showed Brownlee and Massett that if Fluff traveled fourteen hundred miles in the direction he had started he would have to do the last two hundred miles as a swim, because he would strike the Atlantic Ocean at the twelve hundredth mile. But Brownlee just turned up his nose and sneered. He said Fluff was no fool, and that when he reached the coast he would veer to the north and travel along the beach for two hundred miles or so. Then Massett said that he had been thinking about Brownlee's theory, and he *knew* no dog could do what Brownlee said Fluff would do—sixty miles an hour. He said he agreed that a dog like Fluff could do thirty miles an hour if he did not stop to howl, because his howl represented about sixty horse power, but that no dog could ever do sixty miles an hour. Then Brownlee got mad and said Massett was a born idiot, and that Fluff not only *could* do sixty miles, but he could keep on increasing his speed at the rate of thirty miles per gun indefinitely. Then they went home mad, but they agreed to be on hand when Fluff returned. But they were not. Fluff came home in twenty-four hours, almost to the minute.

When I went over and told Brownlee, he wouldn't believe it at first, but when I showed him Fluff, he cheered up and clapped me on the back.

"I tell you," he exclaimed, "we have made a great discovery. We have discovered the law of scared dogs. 'A dog is scared in inverse ratio to the number of guns!' Now, it wouldn't be fair to try Fluff again without giving him a breathing spell, but to-morrow I will come over, and we will try him with four guns. We will work this thing out thoroughly," he said, "before we write to the Academy of Science, or whatever a person would write to, so that there will be no mistake. Before we give this secret to the world we want to have it complete. We will try Fluff with any number of guns, and with pistols and rifles, and if we can get one we will try him with a cannon. We will keep at it for years and years. You and I will be famous."

I told Brownlee that if he wanted to experiment for years with Fluff he could have him, but that all I wanted was to get rid of him; but Brownlee wouldn't hear of that. He said he would buy Fluff of me if he was rich enough, but that Fluff was so valuable he couldn't think of buying him. He would let me keep him. He said he would be over the next day to try Fluff again.

So the next day he and Murchison and Massett came over and held a consultation on my porch to decide how many guns they would try on Fluff. They could not agree. Massett wanted to try four guns and have Fluff absent only half a day, but Brownlee wanted to have me break my shotgun in two and try that on Fluff. He said that according to the law of scared dogs, a half a gun, working it out by inverse ratio, would keep Fluff away for twice as long as one gun, which would be ninety-six hours; and while they were arguing it out Fluff came around the house unsuspectingly and saw us on the porch. He gave us one startled glance and started north by northeast at what Brownlee said was the most marvelous rate of speed he ever saw. Then he and Massett got down off the porch and looked for guns, but there were none in sight. There wasn't anything that looked the least like a gun. Not even a broomstick. Brownlee said he knew what was the matter—Fluff was having a little practice run to keep in good condition, and would be back in a few hours; but, judging by the look he gave us as he went, I thought he would be gone longer than that.

I could see that Brownlee was worried, and as day followed day without any return of Fluff, Murchison and I tried to cheer him up, showing him how much better we all slept while Fluff was away; but it did not cheer up poor Brownlee. He had set his faith on that dog, and the dog had deceived him. We all became anxious about Brownlee's health—he moped around so; and just when we began to be afraid he was going into a decline he cheered up, and came over as bright and happy as a man could be.

"I told you so!" he exclaimed joyfully, as soon as he was inside my gate. "And it makes me ashamed of myself that I didn't think of it the moment I saw Fluff start off. You will never see that dog again."

I told Brownlee that that was good news, anyway, even if it did upset his law of scared dogs; but he smiled a superior smile.

"Disprove nothing!" he said. "It proves my law. Didn't I say in the first place that the time a dog would be gone was in inverse ratio to the number of guns? Well, the inverse ratio to no guns is infinite time—that is how long Fluff will be gone; that is how long he will run. Why, that dog will never stop running while there is any dog left in him. He can't help it—it is the law of scared dogs."

"Do you mean to say," I asked him, "that that dog will run on and on forever?"

"Exactly!" said Brownlee proudly. "As long as there is a particle of him left he will keep on running. That is the law."

31

Maybe Brownlee was right. I don't know. But what I would like to know is the name of some one who would like a dog that looks like Fluff, and is his size, and that howls like him and that answers to his name. A dog of that kind returned to Murchison's house a long time before infinity, and I would like to get rid of him. Brownlee says it isn't Fluff; that his law couldn't be wrong, and that this is merely a dog that resembles Fluff. Maybe Brownlee is right, but I would like to know some one that wants a dog with a richly melodious voice.

THE END